THE PSYCHOLOGY OF OUR DARK SIDE

Humans' Love Affair with Vampires & Werewolves

THE PSYCHOLOGY OF OUR DARK SIDE

Humans' Love Affair
with Vampires &
Werewolves

by Sheila Stewart

Mason Crest Publishers

MASON CREST PUBLISHERS INC.
370 Reed Road
Broomall, Pennsylvania 19008
(866)MCP-BOOK (toll free)
www.masoncrest.com

First Printing
9 8 7 6 5 4 3 2 1

ISBN (series) 978-1-4222-1801-3
Paperback ISBN (series) 978-1-4222-1954-6

Library of Congress Cataloging-in-Publication Data

Stewart, Sheila, 1975–
 The psychology of our dark side : humans' love affair with vampires and werewolves / by Sheila Stewart.
      p. cm.
Includes bibliographical references and index.
ISBN 978-1-4222-1807-5 (hardcover) — ISBN 978-1-4222-1960-7 (pbk.)
1. Vampires. 2. Werewolves. 3. Superstition—Psychological aspects.. I. Title.
BF1556.S79 2011
398'.45—dc22
                                              2010025294

Produced by Harding House Publishing Service, Inc.
www.hardinghousepages.com
Interior design by MK Bassett-Harvey.
Cover design by Torque Advertising + Design.
Printed in the USA by Bang Printing.

CONTENTS

chapter 1

FEAR OF THE OTHER: FIGHTING THE EVIL

There's a whole lot of scary stuff in the world. We've known that from the time we were little kids and made our moms check the closet and under the bed for monsters. All that darkness had to be hiding something, right?

As we get older, we accept—more or less—that there aren't any monsters under our bed. We know, logically, that our closet in the dark has only the same clothes and clutter that it does when the light is on. And yet . . . Even if we can believe that about our closets, what about dark alleys? What about dense forests and jungles in the middle of the night? Who knows what *that* darkness is hiding?

Plus, the world actually is a pretty scary place sometimes, full of diseases and wars and creepy people doing awful things. But, since we live in a scientific and rational world, we are taught that everything has a perfectly reasonable explanation. Sometimes, though, we just don't understand. Sometimes, things just don't make sense. Sometimes, we think, monsters might really make a lot more sense.

Fear of the Unknown

When it comes right down to it, a lot of the time what we're really afraid of is the Unknown, with a capital U. The scariest thing for most people is not knowing. Someone might tell you she's most afraid of snakes, but really she's afraid because she doesn't know what a snake might do. She imagines a snake might suddenly bite her or try to strangle her. Probably, the snake won't do either of those things, but not knowing and trying to imagine what might happen is often a lot scarier than reality.

Think of hearing about a kid who has disappeared in your town. Nobody knows whether she has run away or been kidnapped or what has happened to her. That's the scary part—not knowing. Because if we knew, we might be able to deal with it, but when we don't know, we're left with a vague sense of badness, wrongness, and just plain scariness. That's why the dark is so scary—because we don't know what might be lurking in it.

What does this have to do with werewolves and vampires? Monsters like werewolves and vampires give faces to our fears.

Imagine a little boy going to bed. He's scared; he feels like something is wrong, but he doesn't know exactly what. Maybe he heard his parents fighting, or maybe he saw something on the news that scared him, or maybe his best friend didn't want to play after school and he doesn't know why. The little boy is too young to figure out that these are the things that are really bothering him. He just has a vague sense of uneasiness, and because he doesn't know where it's coming from,

The fear of snakes is one of the most common of human fears.

the uneasiness grows into a sense of wrongness, which grows into fear. But people don't like being scared of the Unknown. We like to figure things out and put a name to them. So the little boy focuses his fear on his closet. He doesn't do it on purpose; it just happens. The closet door is open a crack, and the little boy can just see the dark line of that space. There could be anything in there, he thinks. He remembers hearing a couple of bigger kids on the bus talking about vampires.

"Vampires don't make any noise when they move," one kid had said. "They're suddenly right behind you and they sink their fangs into your neck and drink your blood. All of your blood."

The little boy is suddenly sure a vampire is hiding in his closet. He *knows* a vampire is in there. He stares at the crack, his heart pounding, trying to see if the closet door is starting to open wider. Suddenly, he can't take it anymore.

"Mommy!" he yells, as loudly as he can—maybe that will keep the vampire in the closet a little longer.

His mother appears at his bedroom door. He sobs that there's a vampire in the closet and it's going to suck his blood. His mother opens the closet door and turns on the light. She picks him up and carries him over so he can see the shirts and shoes and his old train set in a box on the floor. Everything is as it always was, with no vampires at all.

"See," his mother says, "there was nothing to be afraid of."

Almost all of us as children worried about what might be lurking in our closets.

The little boy curls up in his bed again and closes his eyes. The fear drifts back once or twice before he falls asleep, but all he has to do is remember his mother showing him the closet. All his earlier fear, which had taken the shape of the vampire in his closet, is now gone, because there wasn't a vampire there at all.

By naming the Unknown, we are able to deal with it, at least in our own minds.

For long-ago peoples, believing in evil spirits and creatures such as vampires and werewolves helped them explain why and how people got sick or why natural disasters and freak accidents sometimes happened. Their scientific understanding hadn't advanced far enough to discover the real reasons these things happened, and they needed some kind of explanation, so vampires and werewolves were quite useful as a scapegoat.

Having an explanation for why things went wrong also gave people a better feeling of control. If they knew why the crops weren't growing or their children were getting sick, they might be able to do something about it. Folklore traditions about vampires and werewolves grew, offering people a whole list of things they could use to ward off monsters—plants the monsters didn't like, rituals to keep them away, places to be avoided.

Despite all these measures, of course, crops still failed and people still got sick or were killed in accidents. But at least people felt they were doing *something* to keep the evil away. And who knows how many terrible things they had prevented?

Fear of the Other

In the distant past, people might live their lives rarely or never seeing anyone from another ethnic group. Merchants and traders from other lands were foreign and exotic—they were fascinating, but also scary. People liked to tell stories about the strange habits of people from other countries. Even people from other villages were considered a bit odd.

Humans have always divided people up into "us and them." "Us" refers to the good people, the normal people, the people who can be trusted and predicted. "Them," on the other hand, refers to everyone else— those people you can't be too sure about. "They" might be people from another country or ethnic background, people who have different religious beliefs, people who dress or talk or act differently. "They" could be any person or group that is different than you are.

This fear of the Other—those who are different—is really a version of the fear of the Unknown. The reason those people who are different worry us is that we just don't know what they might do. They aren't predictable like "us."

Today, we usually understand that people are people, no matter their race or religion or sexual identity.

When someone is different from ourselves, a stranger to us, we often feel as though they are not merely unknown but also alien, frightening, even threatening.

We know this, but sometimes, when we come across someone we really don't understand, our brains automatically label the person as Other, as Unknown—and therefore as scary. In the past, when people believed that some groups of other people couldn't even be considered human, this happened a lot more, and far too often it led to violence.

In some vampire or werewolf stories, the monster was a foreigner, one of that worrying group of Unknowns. *Dracula*, for example, is the most famous of all the vampire stories. The novel was published in 1897 by Bram Stoker, a man who lived in London, England. *Dracula* tells the story of Jonathan Harker, a young English lawyer who travels to Eastern Europe to meet with Count Dracula about a business matter. Dracula is indeed strange, but Harker tries to go along with it at first. Dracula is a foreigner, after all, and a member of the nobility, and maybe his oddness is just because he has different customs. Of course, Harker soon discovers that Dracula is a blood-drinking vampire. . . .

One of the lessons of *Dracula* is that the Other is dangerous. Count Dracula is charming and a good host, but actually he's a monster. The book plays on one of humanity's darkest fears—that the Other, the Unknown, is really something terrible. Hundreds of years ago, when a stranger came to town, he was looked at with suspicion. Why? Because nobody knew anything about him. If a stranger showed up and then someone's sheep

Today's Monsters

These days, people don't usually go around whispering to each other that they think so-and-so is a vampire or a werewolf. Most people don't believe in them, for one thing. A modern equivalent might be a terrorist. We know terrorists exist, and they're scary and unpredictable. They're dangerous, too, just like the vampires and werewolves of the past. People often forget that terrorists, as scary as they are, are actually human beings, with human reasons for what they're doing.

started to disappear, things were even more suspicious. The stranger could be a werewolf, people would mutter to each other. Why else would the sheep start disappearing just when he had arrived in town?

Werewolves, Vampires, and Religion

A lot of werewolf and vampire stories come from folk legends. They were told around campfires at night, passed along from generation to generation, with little changes and twists made along the way. The stories pulled in the beliefs of the people, and everyone would understand the mythology behind them.

When religions like Christianity and Islam started to spread through Europe and the Middle East hundreds of years ago, they met a lot of people who accepted the new religions but kept on telling the stories they had always told. Religious leaders found folk legends just about impossible to destroy, so they did the only thing they could think of—they adapted them.

The church believed strongly in the battle of good against evil, and the monsters of folk legends gave them a ready-made illustration of that fight. While in earlier tales, the creatures and monsters weren't always exactly evil, now they were described as evil demons, or as people controlled by evil demons. Vampires and werewolves were twisted versions of God's creation, the church said, and that twisting could only have been done by the devil.

People already knew the legends, but the church offered them a further explanation: werewolves and vampires existed because the devil had created them by messing up good things God had created, like people and animals. And the devil had created monsters because he hated God and hated people—because he was evil. Vampires and werewolves had given people a focus for nameless fears, but now the church provided a greater enemy and a greater focus. When people were

Christianity connected moral evil with supernatural images of death.
What had once been only terrifying, now became the devil's work.

fearing vampires or fighting werewolves, religious leaders said, they were really fearing and fighting the devil.

By giving creatures like vampires and werewolves a spiritual reason for existing, the church was also able to offer its own defense. What was the devil the most afraid of? The cross, the church said—and so vampires also cringe away from crosses. Holy water, which has been blessed by a priest, can also harm or destroy a vampire. (Modern vampires, who live in a less religious world, aren't always bothered by crosses and holy water.)

Werewolves seem to be immune to religious symbols, perhaps because they are living creatures instead of undead ones. Still, the church played up the unnaturalness of werewolves, claiming they were people who had made a deal with the devil and lost their humanity. In pagan traditions, holy people could sometimes shape shift into animals because they were so connected to Nature, but for the church, werewolves could only be evil.

Clearly, vampires and werewolves are images of the mysterious and the Unknown. They focus our fears and give them a face. But sometimes, we notice, that face is rather attractive.

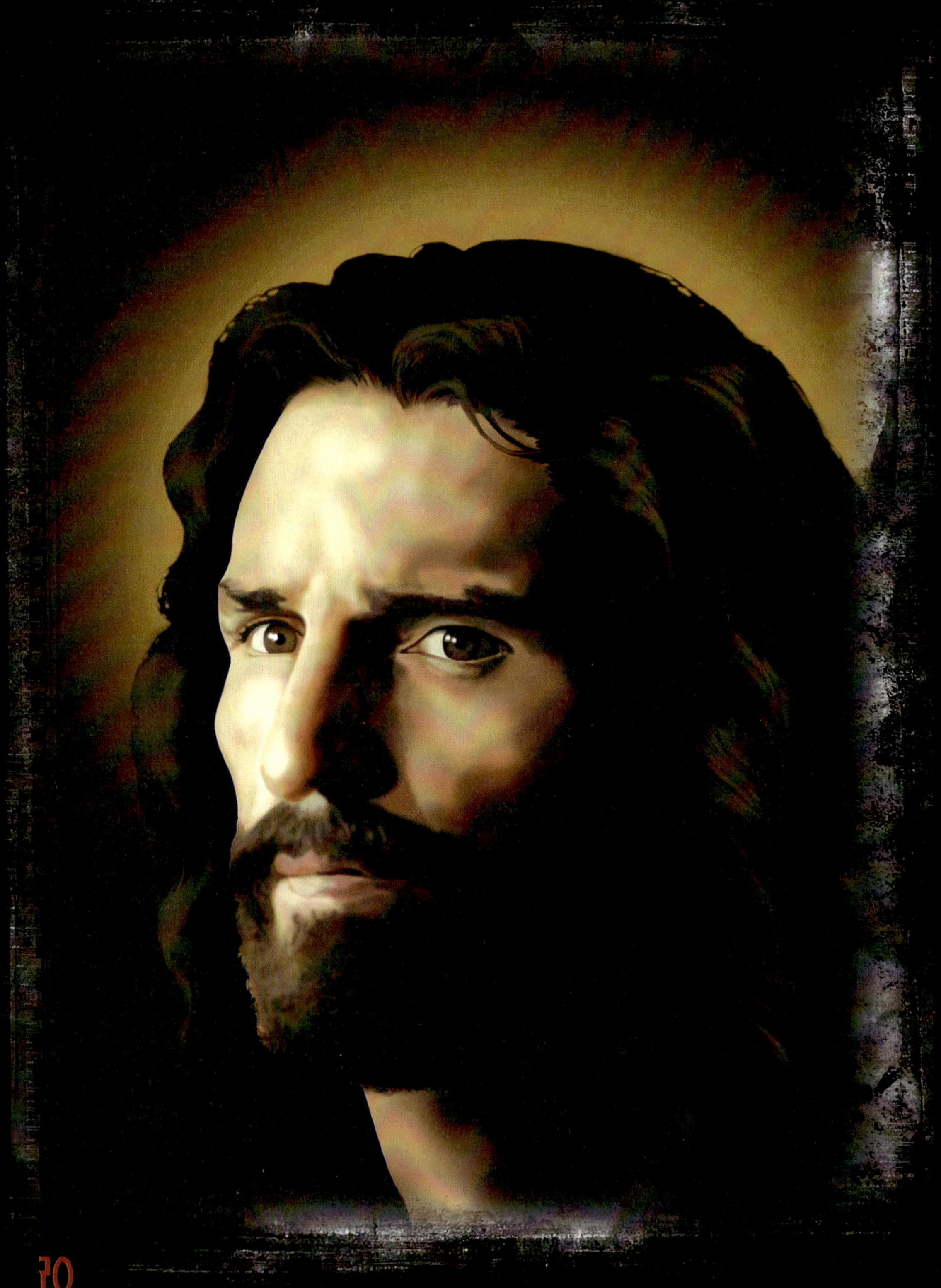

JUDAS AS VAMPIRE

If you are a Christian, what is the worst thing you could possibly do? Well, betray Christ, of course. And if you happened to be alive at the same time as Jesus Christ lived and were one of his best friends but then sold him out for a bit of money to the people who wanted to kill him . . . well, that was very, very bad.

Judas Iscariot was one of the twelve disciples of Jesus Christ. Judas went to the people who hated Jesus and wanted him dead, and offered to turn him over to them if they paid him. They agreed, because this was just the chance they'd been looking for.

After Jesus had been arrested and sentenced to be executed, however, Judas regretted what he had done and hung himself. The Bible doesn't say much more about it than that, but some legends tell how Judas then became a vampire (or the *first* vampire, depending on the story). In these legends, Judas is pretty much the mirror-image opposite of Jesus. Jesus is killed and then comes back to live, alive but with a new and better body. Judas, on the other hand, kills himself and then comes back to life—sort of—as a vampire, one of the living dead.

chapter 2
Attraction to the Other: Vampires, Werewolves, and Sexuality

A brooding, mysterious stranger; a sensuous woman of untold secrets—just because something is strange and different doesn't mean we aren't attracted to it. In fact, sometimes the opposite is true. There's something about the Unknown, with its hints of danger, that can be very interesting. Different people like different things, of course, but risk taking is a very human trait. If someone is attractive enough, a small amount of uncertainty, danger, and risk can make him even more fascinating. (Think of it as adding a little salt to your food!) That's not to say that people are generally attracted to truly hideous scary things. People like their monsters beautiful.

The Byronic Hero

One of the first character types in this dangerous-yet-very-attractive theme is the Byronic hero. Named for the type of characters written about by George Gordon,

In his day, Lord Byron was thought to be dangerously attractive to women.

LORD BYRON AS VAMPIRE

Byron himself had many of the characteristics of the Byronic hero. He was a moody rebel who left a trail of broken hearts behind him. If Byron lived today, he would definitely be someone we'd been seeing on the cover of People magazine and reading about in the entertainment news. Good-looking, fascinating, and eccentric, Lord Byron was famous for being dangerous-yet-attractive. He was always being mixed up in one scandal or another, and one woman whom he'd had an affair with became so obsessed with him that she basically became the first recorded stalker in history. (She famously called him "mad, bad, and dangerous to know"!)

Dr. John Polidori worked as Byron's personal doctor for a while, but he grew to hate his patient so much that he later wrote a short story called "The Vampyre," in which the antagonist, Lord Ruthven, is based on Byron. Polidori's Lord Ruthven is an evil vampire, but women seem helplessly attracted to him. He seduces the women and then kills them, while the frustrated hero is unable to do anything to stop him. To Polidori, Lord Byron looked a lot like a vampire.

Lord Byron, a British poet who lived in the late eighteenth and early nineteenth centuries (as well as for Byron himself), a Byronic hero is a man who is, more or less:

- moody
- a rebel; outside of society
- passionate
- intelligent
- proud and arrogant
- refined, cultured, and sophisticated
- mysterious, charismatic, and attractive
- troubled, cynical, and self-destructive

Ever since he was first created, the Byronic hero has been a part of literature. He shows up in romance novels, in Gothic literature, and in most of the vampire stories from the second half of the twentieth century onward. Which just goes to show how much people like a little mystery and danger in their fantasy relationships.

The Femme Fatale

While the Byronic hero is strictly male, his female counterpart is the femme fatale. The femme fatale is a dangerous woman (the French phrase literally means "deadly woman"), but she is irresistible to men. The idea

of the femme fatale has been around for a very long time. In fact, the first femme fatale was thought to be Lilith, who, according to legend, was the first wife of Adam, before Eve was created. (So, in other words, she was the first woman on Earth.) According to the stories, Lilith considered herself an equal to Adam in all things, including sexually. In a time when meek, submissive women were considered to be "good women," Lilith represented the bold, bad woman—definitely interesting to men, but also threatening and frightening.

At the time these legends were being told, people believed that the world was supposed to have a certain order and hierarchy. Angels were higher than people, for example, and people were higher than animals. And men were higher than women. Women were expected to "know their place." They were supposed to obey men and not try to control them. Femmes fatales were women who didn't buy into that. They were dangerous because they didn't want men to control them and instead, used their sexuality to control men. In fact, by not willingly taking their place in the order of creation, femmes fatales were thought to threaten the very stability of the world. They were seen as completely evil.

Still, evil or not, femmes fatales were very attractive. In the distinction between "the girl you want to date" and "the girl you want to marry," a femme fatale would definitely be in the first category. A femme fatale was dangerous and exciting. But, of course, no man would

Screen Vamps

In the early nineteenth century, in the days of silent films, the "vamp" was a well-known character. The vamp short for vampiress was a seductive femme fatale. She was often portrayed as a mysterious foreign woman and was the direct opposite of the fresh-faced, wholesome woman that the hero should be falling for. Actress Theda Bara often played the vamp in silent movies and was so successful at it that nobody wanted to cast her as any other type of character.

Theda Bara did goth before anyone else did!

want to end up married to her, since she wouldn't ever agree to let him control her.

Vampires and femmes fatales were connected very early on in the folklore. Lilith, as a consequence of refusing to submit to Adam, was thought to have become a kind of demon. Sometimes she is described as eating young babies or killing women in childbirth. Sometimes she is a succubus and preys on men. A succubus is similar to a vampire, but instead of drinking blood she drains the life force of a man. She comes to a man in his sleep and has sex with him, leaving him weakened and drained.

Femmes fatales are sometimes actually called vampires, or sexual vampires. This underlines how dangerous they are, but it still doesn't take away from how attractive they are. Rudyard Kipling wrote a poem in 1897 called "The Vampire," about a man who is brought down by a femme fatale. The woman in the poem isn't the blood-sucking type of vampire, but she uses the man who has fallen in love with her ("But the fool he called her his lady fair") and leaves him a shell of his former self ("So some of him lived but the most of him died").

Want to Date a Vampire?

So what about those people who wish they could date a vampire—a real, blood-drinking vampire, not just someone who is going to drain your energy? Why is that? Is it because the vampire has put a spell on them to make them fall in love? Maybe. Sometimes that's the case in stories, but somebody would have to have dumped a vampire love potion in the water supply to explain the major obsession with vampires that seems to be going around these days.

An article in *Psychology Today* explains the attraction with descriptions of biological programming (what our bodies tell us we should be looking for in a mate) and neurotransmitters. It also quotes a psychologist, Michael Cunningham, as saying that vampire romances give women a chance to get to know what goes inside men: "The vampires that populate these dark fantasy worlds mirror the men of the real world: complex, suffering creatures who must battle their warring impulses to harm and to protect, and who need women to recognize their torment, care about them, and trust them."

The article has a lot of truth in it, but it doesn't explain why people—women especially—seem to be attracted to vampires (creatures who want to drink their blood) and not just dark, brooding Byronic heroes.

Books, movies, and television shows that take us away from our real lives and allow us to experience things we won't really get to do are known as escapist fiction. A lot of escapist fiction gives people the chance to experience things they wouldn't even *want* to do in real life. And yet a little part of them *does* want to do it, *does* want to experience the excitement portrayed.

Have you ever watched an action movie? Exciting as it is to watch people jumping out of airplanes and being shot at, we wouldn't really want those things to happen to us. That would be *too* scary. So, by reading and watching escapist fiction, we feed that part of us that is attracted to danger.

The character of the Byronic hero is part of escapist fiction. In the 1960s and '70s, when women were breaking out of their traditional roles, "bodice-ripper" romance novels were very popular. The men in these novels were very much the Byronic hero. They were dangerous, sexy, and didn't take no for an answer. In real life, the women who read these books would have probably hated a man who pushed them around like the heroes in the novels did to the heroines. Women were becoming liberated, but there was some small part of them that still wanted a man to take charge.

Those novels are still around today, although they aren't as popular as they once were. Instead, vampire novels have become popular. Why? Well, having the hero be a vampire pushes the fantasy one step further from reality. A lot of women can read the old bodice-rippers and clearly see that the men in them were jerks. Just because it's fiction doesn't make that any less true. But if the hero is a vampire, he can be just as attractive and yet have an excuse for his aggressive behavior. The vampire-hero isn't evil, after all, and he struggles with his blood urges. Having him struggle on behalf

HOMOSEXUALITY AND VAMPIRES

A 2001 article in **The Advocate**, a national gay and lesbian magazine, claims that "vampires have always held irresistible appeal for queer readers." The article goes on to discuss homoeroticism in vampire fiction: "When you think of a man who dresses well, stays out late, and has an endless appetite for supple young flesh, admit it: **Vampire** is the second thing that comes to mind." Katherine Ramsland, in her book *Piercing the Darkness: Undercover with Vampires in America Today*, also noticed the attraction vampires seemed to hold for gay men, "in part because they view the vampire as transcending gender and lacking in culturally imposed prejudice with regard to choice of victim. Vampires also captured the unrelenting sensuality that gay men have told me they love."

This, of course, is a generalization—some gay men prefer werewolves.

of a woman is a very appealing trait for readers. And, because vampires aren't real, many women feel better about enjoying their fictional heroes' aggressive natures.

What About Werewolves?

When people think about sexy supernatural creatures, why is it that they usually think of vampires a long time before they think about werewolves? Of course, that might be changing, due to the character of Jacob in Stephanie Meyer's *Twilight* books. Jacob is a werewolf, and a very good-looking one at that.

The trouble with werewolves is that they have traditionally been portrayed as ordinary humans (usually men) who, through some unfortunate happening, have been transformed into wolves. When an unfortunate transformation creates a vampire, the vampire is always a vampire after that and can learn to control himself (if that's what the plot of story requires). But most werewolf stories have shown werewolves as being unable to control their transformations and unable to control themselves while in wolf form. So a werewolf might be absolutely gorgeous and a great guy as a human, but when he transforms into his wolf form (usually when the moon is full or else when emotions are high), he might kill and eat you and not even know it was you. That's not a very attractive trait.

Jacob in Twilight is an attractive werewolf!

the TWILIGHT saga

new moon

Oz, from *Buffy the Vampire Slayer*, transforms into a werewolf in the days around the full moon. Because he has no control over his actions when he is in wolf form, he allows himself to be locked up before his transformation. In this way, he makes sure nobody gets hurt. This allowed him to play a romantic part in the plot and not immediately kill his girlfriend.

In the newest werewolf stories, including the *Twilight* books, werewolves are often able to transform at will (although usually this is something they have to learn). Modern werewolves can also usually control themselves while in their wolf forms. This makes them much better candidates for romance.

While the darkness we see in others can be either frightening or attractive or both, what about the darkness we find within ourselves? Do we fear it and try to get rid of it? Or do we embrace the darkness?

38.

chapter 3
OUR DARK SELVES

Everybody has a dark side. Think about it: does everyone know exactly what you're like? Or do you want to hide some things from some people—or from almost everybody? Are there some things you don't even want to admit to yourself?

The psychologist Carl Jung wrote about something he called the shadow. The shadow is the dark side of the personality, with all the stuff we don't want to think about. Some people deny they actually have a dark side, while others deal with it by projecting it onto other people—which means that they see and dislike things about other people that they are trying to hide about themselves. Jung thought the best way to deal with our shadow side was to face it. He believed people should examine themselves thoroughly and acknowledge all the good and bad parts. But, he said, most people do not have the courage to do that.

Embracing Our Wild Side

Everybody has roles to play. Some of them you choose, and some you find yourself in. You might choose to be a member of the basketball team or choose to get a job at the local bookstore. Roles like daughter or son, sister or brother, or high school student were not ones you chose, though. But however you acquired your roles, each comes with its own set of expectations. If you are on the basketball team, for example, you are expected to go to practices, to keep in shape, and to not do anything that would harm the team's reputation.

Roles and expectations are a part of life. They help keep society going. Without them, there would chaos. In some cases, the expectations or the roles need to be changed. The feminist movement, for example, challenged the idea that women were supposed to be passive and obedient, to not work outside of the home, vote, or wear certain clothes. The gay rights movement challenges the idea that homosexuality is something to be ignored, shunned, or cured.

Whether or not the roles you have create expectations that are unreasonable or just plain wrong, expectations can still start to chafe sometimes. "The modern woman is a blur of activity," writes Clarissa Pinkola Estés. "She is pressured to be all things to all people." This pressure is true for both men and women. We become so focused on trying to meet everybody's expectations

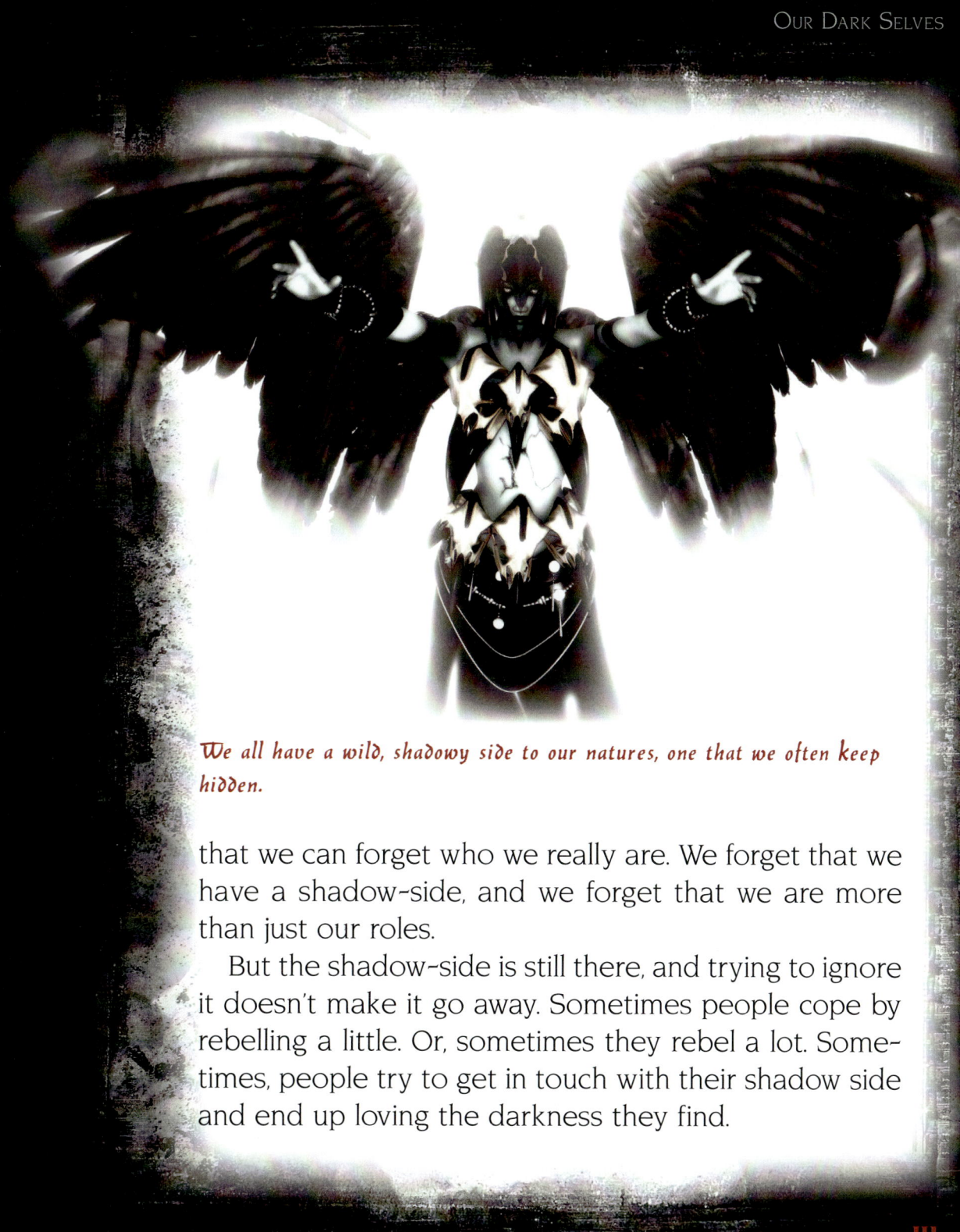

We all have a wild, shadowy side to our natures, one that we often keep hidden.

that we can forget who we really are. We forget that we have a shadow-side, and we forget that we are more than just our roles.

But the shadow-side is still there, and trying to ignore it doesn't make it go away. Sometimes people cope by rebelling a little. Or, sometimes they rebel a lot. Sometimes, people try to get in touch with their shadow side and end up loving the darkness they find.

Clarissa Pinkola Estés, in her book *Women Who Run With the Wolves*, writes:

> We are all filled with a longing for the wild. There are few culturally sanctioned antidotes for this yearning. We were taught to feel shame for such a desire. We grew our hair long and used it to hide our feelings. But the shadow of Wild Woman still lurks behind us during our days and in our nights. No matter where we are, the shadow that trots behind us is definitely four-footed.

Werewolves and vampires are images of our dark side. They embody the things we keep hidden. We love them partly because we see ourselves in them—the parts of ourselves that scare us but that are wild and real and need to be acknowledged.

What Is Normal?

People want to belong. They want to feel understood and loved and accepted. They want to be part of a group. But people also want to be individuals. They don't want to be lost in the crowd. With the help of the Internet, people today can be complete individuals in their homes and schools but also find groups of others online just like them to love and accept them. Personalization and individualization are available for your computer, your car, your clothes, and anything else you like.

Back in the 1940s and '50s, conformity was what was valued. In those days, people who did not fit in were seen as social outcasts, and there was a lot of pressure to look like everyone else and not do anything too weird. That's not to say people didn't find ways to explore their dark sides and be individuals, but in general they did try to keep those parts of themselves quieter.

Society seems to have come a long way since then, but really, we just have a larger tolerance for what is seen as "normal." Different styles of clothes and hair, different types of music, different sizes and colors of cars—people have a lot of choices these days. We tend to categorize people based on the kinds of things they choose, but in the twenty-first century a lot more things fit into the larger "normal" category than they once did.

BERSERKERS

Among the Norse Viking warriors were a special type of warrior called berserkers. In battle, the berserkers were extremely fierce. They often wore bear or wolf skins and seemed to take on the qualities of those animals. Their strength seemed superhuman, they ignored wounds and injuries, and they were sometimes so crazed with battle that they howled, foamed at the mouth, and bit their shields. Some historians think the berserkers took some kind of hallucinogenic drug before battles, in order to send themselves into their blood-rages. A few, however, prefer to believe that they were actually werewolves or were-bears.

No matter how large that "normal" category is, though, there are going to be people who don't want to be inside it. And even with the wider tolerance of the twenty-first century, most people would consider certain behaviors or styles to be just a little weird.

What about people who see themselves as being real vampires or real werewolves? Do these people fall into

What is the most secret part of you, the part you keep hidden from others? Fantasy is one way people explore the parts of themselves that seem less normal.

Raised by Wolves

Stories have been told for thousands of years about lost or abandoned children who were taken in by animals. Usually the animals are wolves, but in some stories they are bears, apes, or even gazelles. The children in these situations grow up in tune with nature and with their wild sides, but they are not so much in tune with their humanity. If these feral children are taken out of the wild, they often have difficulty adjusting to humans and human society.

the category of "normal"? And does it even matter if they do or not? Some of these people are clearly unusual and clearly don't fit in with most of society's groups, but others are professional businesspeople or hardworking cashiers or factory workers. They live one life in "normal" society and another—hidden—life on their own time.

Why Be a Vampire?

When people say they are a real vampire, what do they mean? And why would they even want to be a real vampire?

Different people mean different things by "real vampire," first of all. Some mean those who choose to drink blood. Some mean those who have to drink blood. Others mean those who don't drink blood at all, but instead consume energy, or life force, from other people.

As to why someone would want to be a vampire, there are likely a thousand different reasons for a thousand different people. Some who study the vampire subcultures have linked the attraction to having been abused as a child. Katherine Ramsland, a journalist who wrote a book about the vampire culture, says, "The vampire appears to be a means of self-reinvention for those who wish to cut themselves off from a family or culture that they disown, and to rediscover themselves purely as individuals."

Some who identify with vampires are drawn to their darkness, which mirrors that in their own selves. Mark Spivey writes about the connection between GenXers and vampires, talking about their attraction to the vampires in the novels of Anne Rice:

> GenXers are desperately out of control and lack power for their lives and futures—in their minds at least. The vampire represents the power, the control over circumstances and the sensuality that elude them.... The vampire existence, as depicted, is a very real description of the typical GenX lifestyle: dark, mysterious outcasts who subsist on

society's blood, feeding when and where they can to survive—and survive they will at all costs. When the magic is drained from life, the spiritual vortex begins to swirl. Vampires become the junk-food spirituality for the hungry.

The connections Spivey makes between vampires and GenXers can also be made between vampires and

I WANT TO LIVE FOREVER

Immortality is one of the perks of being a vampire, and it is certainly something pursued by scientists and people in general. While scientists study the genes that cause aging and try to find a "cure" for death, millions of people spend millions of dollars on plastic surgery, botox treatments, and other methods to make them look younger. If science suddenly discovered that vampires were real, you could bet that some people would be lining up to be turned, just so they wouldn't have to worry about getting old.

those in more recent generations. Each generation creates its own images of power, finding in them both the darkness they are being told to repress and the power they long to experience.

Vampires are powerful beings, and when someone doesn't have much power in mainstream society they might be attracted to something like vampires. Vampires, after all, are outcasts, but they are also beautiful, charismatic, and very powerful.

Why Be a Werewolf?

Do people want to be real werewolves, as some want to be real vampires? And, if so, are they attracted to werewolves for the same reasons as people are attracted to vampires? Well, the reasons are similar, if not exactly the same. Wanting to be a werewolf or a vampire can both come out of a feeling of not fitting in with society. Finding others who feel the same way gives a sense of belonging.

Groups of "real werewolves" seem to be a more recent phenomenon than "real vampires." Could it be that the popularity of environmentalism in the twenty-first century leaves people with a longing for a deeper connection with Nature? Wolves are wild and free, and we long for that too.

A news station in San Antonio, Texas, recently aired a story about teens who dress up like wolves and band together in packs. The news anchors seemed bemused by the teens, but they agreed that everyone needs to belong. The teens in the pack consider each other family, and depend on each other for support. Some in the pack seem to think dressing up like wolves is merely something that indicates the group is connected to each other—a mark of belonging—while others believe they are truly part-wolf. One member, Deikitsen Wolfram Lupus, says, "I don't believe anyone is just human. Everyone's got something else mixed in with them. They just have to look inside themselves and find out what it is." The connection between human beings and nature comes much more easily for young people today than for many in past generations.

Across the Internet, teens and tweens are discussing seriously how to shift into a wolf state, drawing distinctions between m-shifting (mental shifting) and p-shifting (physical shifting). In m-shifting, a person gets into the mindset of being a wolf, or simply feels a little wolfish. P-shifting, on the other hand, means changing physically into a wolf, although it very rarely means a complete transformation into wolf-form. More often, it means the werewolf has changed her heart rate, dilated her pupils, or raised her body temperature.

Whether or not these teens truly believe they have a wolf-form, they are clearly finding a sense of belonging in their online or real-life wolf packs. Belonging to a group is one of the strongest of human longings. Asserting your individuality is another strong drive. As part of a werewolf pack, people can sometimes find both.

So is all this attraction to vampires and werewolves about finding and embracing our dark sides, our wild sides? Or can we integrate our humanity with our inner darkness?

THE DARKEST OF THE DARK

Sometimes, people go too far into the dark of their souls. Sometimes the darkness overwhelms the light. People such as the famous historical vampire, Vlad the Impaler, or the Blood Countess Elizabeth Bathory, murdered hundreds, perhaps thousands, of people, and found themselves loving the darkness far too much. People who are serial killers, sadists, and torturers embrace the darkness within themselves. Unlike most people, the small hidden part in *these* people's personality is the good, the compassionate, and the loving.

chapter 4

INTO THE LIGHT: REDEMPTION

Is having an interest in vampires and werewolves really all about embracing our dark side? In the vampire and werewolf stories from the nineteenth and early twentieth centuries, the creatures were almost always bad—and they were almost always thought of as "creatures." Today, the vampires and werewolves seem a lot more like real people. They're troubled, moody, have relationship problems, and would rather be a hero than a villain.

What has changed over the course of the twentieth century to cause this shift in our fictional monsters?

Postmodernism

People aren't certain about much these days. We could blame Einstein and quantum mechanics for that—after all, Einstein told us the universe was built on uncertainty and probability rather than cold, hard facts and absolute distinctions. Many people had trouble accepting that idea at first, but by the end of the twentieth century, it was just part of life and we didn't think about it much. Of course, most people don't spend a lot of time thinking about the underlying workings of the universe, but it's true that the general idea of uncertainty has entered our culture.

We don't like black and white these days. We see all too clearly that shades of gray are mixed up in everything we do. Postmodernism is a description of this way of thinking. According to postmodernism, there isn't any such thing as absolutes of right and wrong or answers that work for everybody at any time. Postmodernists don't have a lot of answers, but they do have a lot of questions. In fact, any answer they do give might start with, "It depends . . ."

In a postmodern world, how could we possibly label all vampires and werewolves as evil, simply because they happen to be vampires or werewolves? It makes much more sense that, even if some vampires and werewolves might *tend* toward evil, there would likely be some (or at least one) who were good. Or at least more good than evil.

And so we have vampires like Angel, from *Buffy the Vampire Slayer*, who try to make up for their earlier evil deeds by saving lives instead of taking them. Vampires like Nick, from *Forever Knight*, and Mick, from *Moonlight*, who work to solve crimes and just don't tell most people about their true nature. And the vampires and werewolves from the *Twilight* series, who have the varied personalities of non-supernatural humans. Being a vampire or a werewolf doesn't automatically mean anything these days. It's just another of those traits that some people have and some people don't.

Tolerance and Diversity

These days, we're used to being tolerant about people who are different from ourselves. Or, if we aren't actually tolerant about everybody, we're at least used to the idea that we're *supposed* to be. Diversity is a good thing and we learn from other cultures. "It's not right, it's not wrong, it's just different" is the motto exchange students are taught. And it's an important lesson to learn.

Existing on the margins of society, vampires and werewolves function as images of other groups that have traditionally been pushed out of mainstream culture. Perhaps this also explains the appeal these stories have for members of the GLBT community. Like gays, lesbians, bisexuals, and transgendered people throughout history, vampires and werewolves have been condemned, hunted, feared, and shunned. The emergence of vampires and werewolves into mainstream society, as depicted in shows like *True Blood*, mirrors the emergence of the GLBT community. In both cases, some people are very against the coming out, while others are supportive.

The same parallels can be drawn with any other traditionally marginalized group. The most modern stories of vampires and werewolves are stories of tolerance and acceptance and the difficulties involved in achieving that status.

Everyone Needs Hope

Without hope, people get sick and die and nobody feels like getting up in the morning. Hope is a necessary part of life. We understand this, although sometimes we call it something else—like having a purpose or having a goal or being optimistic or having determination.

The older vampire and werewolf stories were stories about monsters. They were stories about the evil in the world and all the bad things we don't really understand. In those stories, the evil can come right up and take over your mother or child or best friend, transforming them into something evil and awful. The good people in those stories killed the monsters, or tried to at least. The meaning of those stories was about fighting evil, getting rid of it, and making the world a better and safer place.

Today, werewolves and vampires struggle to find their place in the world. We see them as human these days. And we have all those shades of gray to take into

VAMPIRES, WEREWOLVES, AND TEENAGE HORMONES

In some of the newer vampire and werewolf stories–including the **Twilight** series–the idea of restraint plays a big role. When supernatural boys have relationships with human girls, they can be tempted to bite them, something their vampire or werewolf side tells them to do. (This can be true for supernatural girls and human boys, too, but it comes up less often in the stories.) In a very similar way, fully human teenagers can find their hormones raging, although the pull is toward sex, not biting.

account. We don't want to believe that someone could be completely evil, without any hope of redemption.

Today's vampire stories are just as much about fighting evil and making the world a better and safer place as were the old stories. But while the old stories fought evil by killing the monsters, the new ones fight evil by overcoming the darkness within the monsters. This is not to say that all the vampires and werewolves and the evil human people in the world will turn good, but

Despite their attraction to the dark, humans also have hope that one day they will be able to reconcile the light and the darkness, and regain their lost innocence.

we need to know there is always hope. To be good or evil is a choice, whether someone is human, vampire, or werewolf, and there is always hope for redemption, no matter how dark things look.

Words You May Not Know

chafe: To irritate or make sore by rubbing against something.

chaos: A state of extreme confusion and disorder.

charismatic: Extraordinarily attractive, as in someone with a magnetic personality.

conformity: The condition where everything is exactly the same.

cynical: Believing the worst about reality.

hierarchy: A series of ordered groupings within a system.

GenX: The generation of people born between 1961 and 1981.

Gothic: A style of literature that focused on dark, spooky, romantic settings and characters.

marginalized: Pushed to the side of society, left out of the mainstream.

neurotransmitters: The chemicals within the brain that help carry messages between nerve cells.

passive: Unable or unwilling to take action.

rational: Sensible, having to do with the mind's abilities to order the world.

sadists: People who enjoy hurting others.

sanctioned: Officially approved.

scapegoat: Someone or something that bears the sins and guilt of others.

sensuous: Taking delight in physical beauty and pleasure.

submissive: Willing to give in to the wishes and commands of others.

vortex: A whirlpool or whirlwind.

Find Out More on the Internet

The Allure of the Vampire
www.dvorkin.com/essays/vampallure.htm

Monstrous Vampires
vampires.monstrous.com

Monstrous Werewolves
werewolves.monstrous.com

Vampires
www.vampires.com

Werewolf
www.crystalinks.com/werewolves.html

The Werewolf and Shapeshifter Codex
yaiolani.tripod.com/handbook.htm

Further Reading

Curran, Bob. *Werewolves: A Guide to Shapeshifters, Lycanthropes, and Man-Beasts*. Franklin Lakes, N.J.: Career Press, 2009.

Cybulski, Angela. *Werewolves: Fact or Fiction?* San Diego, Cal.: Greenhaven, 2004.

Godfrey, Linda S. *Werewolves: Mysteries, Legends, and Unexplained Phenomena*. New York: Checkmark Books, 2008.

Hallab, Mary Y. *Vampire God: The Allure of the Undead in Western Culture*. Albany, N.Y.: SUNY Press, 2009.

Housel, Rebecca, and J. Jeremy Wisnewski, eds. *Twilight and Philosophy: Vampires, Vegetarians, and the Pursuit of Immortality*. Hoboken, N.J.: John Wiley & Sons, 2009.

Regan, Sally. *The Vampire Book*. New York: DK, 2009.

Bibliography

Allen, Rosemary A. "The Byronic Hero," web.archive.org/web/20080209183109/http://spider.georgetowncollege.edu/english/allen/byron2.htm (10 June 2010).

Arthen, Inanna. "Real Vampires." *FireHeart* 2(Fall/Winter 1988–89) www.earthspirit.com/fireheart/fhvampire.html (13 June 2010).

Berreby, David. *Us and Them: Understanding Your Tribal Mind*. New York: Little, Brown and Company, 2005.

Chen, Sophie. "Bloodlust: Why Women Are Suckers for Bloodsuckers." *Psychology Today* Nov/Dec 2009: pg 18.

Conger, Joe. "Did You Miss the Buzz? Teen Wolves Descend Upon San Antonio High Schools." 27 May 2010. KENS-5, www.kens5.com/home/Teen-wolves-in-San-Antonio-94015234.html (11 June 2010).

Editors of Time-Life. *Transformations: Mysteries of the Unknown.* Alexandria, Va.: Time-Life Books, 1989.

Estés, Clarissa Pinkola. *Women Who Run With the Wolves: Myths and Stories of the Wild Woman Archetype.* New York: Ballantine Books, 1992.

Feist, Jess. "Jung: Analytical Psychology." *Theories of Personality, Third Edition.* Fort Worth, Texas: Harcourt Brace, 1994.

Jones, Wenzel. "Vamping It Up." *The Advocate* 6 Nov. 2001, pg. 48.

Lecouteux, Claude. *Witches, Werewolves, and Fairies: Shapeshifters and Astral Doubles in the Middle Ages.* Rochester, Vt.: Inner Traditions, 2003.

Ramsland, Katherine. *Piercing the Darkness: Undercover with Vampires in America Today.* New York: HarperPrism, 1998.

Webb, L.J. "The Byronic Vampire." *Crede Byron: Byron & Newstead Abbey,* www.praxxis.co.uk/credebyron/vampyre.htm (10 June 2010).

Williams, John. "Meaning Wolf: All Cultures Have Myths That Embody a Basic Belief System About Nature." 1996. Wolf Song of Alaska, www.wolfsongalaska.org/wolves_and_religion_meaning_wolf.html (8 June 2010).

Witcombe, Christopher L.C.E. "Eve and the Identity of Women: Eve & Lilith," 2000, witcombe.sbc.edu/eve-women/7evelilith.html (11 June 2010).

Index

About The Author

Sheila Stewart has written several dozen books for young people. She has a master's degree in English literature and currently works as a writer and editor. She lives in the Southern Tier of New York State with her two young children, for whom she fights monsters regularly.

Picture Credits